Reading tips

This book focuses on two sounds made with the letter e: e as in bed and ee as in he.

Tricky words in this book

Any words in bold may have unusual spellings or are new and have not yet been introduced.

Tricky word in this book:

scheming

Extra ways to have fun with this book

After the reader has read the story, ask them questions about what they have just read:

What kind of animal was Meg?
Can you remember two words that contain the different sounds shown by the letter e?

I could be Superhero Ed's companion, Sidekick Fred!

A pronunciation guide

This grid contains the sounds used in the stories in levels 4, 5 and 6 and a guide on how to say them. /a/ represents the sounds made, rather than the letters in a word.

/ai/ as in game	/ai/ as in play/they	/ee/ as in leaf/these	/ee/ as in he
/igh/ as in kite/light	/igh/ as in find/sky	/oa/ as in home	/oa/ as in snow
/oa/ as in cold	/y+oo/ as in cube/music/new	long /oo/ as in flute/crew/blue	/oi/ as in boy
/er/ as in bird/hurt	/or/ as in snore/oar/door	/or/ as in dawn/sauce/walk	/e/ as in head
/e/ as in said/any	/ou/ as in cow	/u/ as in touch	/air/ as in hare/bear/there
/eer/ as in deer/here/cashier	/t/ as in tripped/skipped	/d/ as in rained	/j/ as in gent/gin/gym
/j/ as in barge/hedge	/s/ as in cent/circus/cyst	/s/ as in prince	/s/ as in house
/ch/ as in itch/catch	/w/ as in white	/h/ as in who	/r/ as in write/rhino

Superhero Ed

Level 6B

Written by Louise Goodman
Illustrated by Kimberley Scott

What is synthetic phonics?

Synthetic phonics teaches children to recognise the sounds of letters and to blend (synthesise) them together to make whole words.

Understanding sound/letter relationships gives children the confidence and ability to read unfamiliar words, without having to rely on memory or guesswork; this helps them to progress towards independent reading.

Did you know? Spoken English uses more than 40 speech sounds. Each sound is called a *phoneme*. Some phonemes relate to a single letter (d-o-g) and others to combinations of letters (sh-ar-p). When a phoneme is written down it is called a *grapheme*. Teaching these sounds, matching them to their written form and sounding out words for reading is the basis of synthetic phonics.

Consultant

I love reading phonics has been created in consultation with language expert Abigail Steel. She has a background in teaching and teacher training and is a respected expert in the field of synthetic phonics. Abigail Steel is a regular contributor to educational publications. Her international education consultancy supports parents and teachers in the promotion of literacy skills.

Sounds in this story are
highlighted in the grid.

		/ul/ as in pencil/ hospital	/z/ as in fries/ cheese/breeze
/f/ as in phone	/f/ as in rough		
/n/ as in knot/ gnome/engine	/m/ as in welcome /thumb/column	/g/ as in guitar/ghost	/zh/ as in vision/beige
/k/ as in chord	/k/ as in plaque/ bouquet	/nk/ as in uncle	/ks/ as in box/books/ ducks/cakes
/a/ and /o/ as in hat/what	/e/ and /ee/ as in bed/he	/i/ and /igh/ as in fin/find	/o/ and /oa/ as in hot/cold
/u/ and short /oo/ as in but/put	/ee/, /e/ and /ai/ as in eat/ bread/break	/igh/, /ee/ and /e/ as in tie/field/friend	/ou/ and /oa/ as in cow/blow
/ou/, /oa/ and /oo/ as in out/ shoulder/could	/i/ and /ai/ as in money/they	/c/ and /s/ as in cat/cent	/y/, /igh/ and /i/ as in yes/sky/myth
/g/ and /j/ as in got/giant	/ch/, /c/ and / sh/ as in chin/ school/chef	/er/, /air/ and /eer/ as in earth/bear/ears	/u/, /ou/ and /oa/ as in plough/dough

Be careful not to add an 'uh' sound to 's', 't', 'p',
'c', 'h', 'r', 'm', 'd', 'g', 'l', 'f' and 'b'. For example,
say 'fff' not 'fuh' and 'sss' not 'suh'.

Ed was the best superhero you've ever met. He had a special red vest and cape with sequins.

He could fight baddies and save the world! The worst baddie was Wicked Ted. He was a **scheming** villain.

One day Superhero Ed heard a yell.
He jumped the bed...
He jumped the desk...
He even jumped the fence!

"What's wrong, Deb?"

"Wicked Ted has taken Emu Meg.
I don't know where they could be!
Help me, I beg you!" she said.

Superhero Ed followed the
trail. It led to a dead end. Then
Superhero Ed saw Wicked Ted
with Emu Meg.

They were in a plane!
Superhero Ed jumped the wall...
He jumped the lamp post...
He even jumped the tree!

The plane landed in the sea.
Wicked Ted jumped onto a boat!

Superhero Ed grabbed Emu Meg,
but just then the boat rocked...

...and they all fell in!
"Help! I can't swim!" cried
Wicked Ted.

"Neither can I!" said Superhero Ed.
Deb arrived in time.
"I can!" she said.

Deb helped them onto the boat.

"Emu Meg!" she said, giving her a hug.

"Wicked Ted, you must behave!"
she said.
"I'm sorry, I will," said Wicked Ted.

"Thank you Superhero Ed!"
she said.
Superhero Ed just smiled.

Superhero Ed jumped the fence...
He jumped the desk...
And he jumped into bed.
What a busy day for Superhero Ed.

OVER **48** TITLES IN SIX LEVELS
Abigail Steel recommends...

Some titles from Level 4

The Maze	Fairy Fay's Bad Day	Pirate School
978-1-84898-559-9	978-1-84898-560-5	978-1-84898-566-7

Some titles from Level 5

Snapped by Sam	Max's Trip	George the Genius Gerbil
978-1-84898-561-2	978-1-84898-562-9	978-1-84898-567-4

Other titles to enjoy from Level 6

What Wally Wanted	Adine's Igloo	The Robot Bop
978-1-84898-563-6	978-1-84898-569-8	978-1-84898-570-4

An Hachette UK Company
www.hachette.co.uk

Copyright © Octopus Publishing Group Ltd 2012
First published in Great Britain in 2012 by TickTock, an imprint of Octopus Publishing Group Ltd,
Endeavour House, 189 Shaftesbury Avenue, London WC2H 8JY.
www.octopusbooks.co.uk

ISBN 978 1 84898 564 3

Printed and bound in China
10 9 8 7 6 5 4 3 2 1